# THE VERY FIRST THANKSGIVING

*Pioneers on the Rio Grande*

# THE VERY FIRST

by Bea Bragg

illustrated by Antonio Castro

# THANKSGIVING

## *Pioneers on the Rio Grande*

*Harbinger House* ❖ *Tucson*

Designed by Rebecca Gaver

Published by Harbinger House, Inc.,
3131 N. Country Club, Tucson, Arizona 85716

Printed in the United States of America

Library of Congress Cataloging-in-Publication Data

Bragg, Bea, 1914–
The very first Thanksgiving: pioneers on the Rio Grande / by Bea Bragg:
illustrated by Antonio Castro.
p. cm.
Summary: When fourteen-year-old Manuel and his younger brother join a difficult
expedition through the Southwest desert to the Rio Grande in 1598, their comical
trained goat is instrumental in helping them survive.
ISBN 0-943173-22-1:   $7.95
[1. America — Discovery and exploration — Fiction.     2. Explorers — Fiction.
3. Goats — Fiction.]
I. Castro, Antonio, 1941 –     ill.     II. Title.
P27.B7325Ve 1989     [Fic] — dc20     89-15562     CIP     AC

❖

*To my loving family
and to the other,
Manuel Carillo (1906 – 1989)*

❖

M ANUEL LOOKED down the narrow street. Fernando had to come soon. Captain-General Martinez would get so hungry he would pull Tia Margarita's clothes off the fence and eat them again. And one more time of that...Manuel shuddered to think what would happen. For such a talented goat, Captain-General Martinez could be a pain in the neck.

"Manuel! Manuel!" Fernando's shouts came from far down the hilly street. Manuel put his hands over his ears and went inside their hut.

*Would he ever learn?*

"Manuel!" Fernando roared through the door.

"Not so loud, Fernando. You know what Tia Margarita will say. And she'll do more than that. She'll make you clean up her kitchen. And where's the corn for Captain-General Martinez?"

But nothing would calm Fernando.

"Listen, listen, Manuel. They're coming!"

"Who's coming?"

"Don Juan de Oñate! And the horses and the soldiers and the padres and the..."

*Is it really true?* Is the great Don Juan de Oñate finally in Santa Barbara? Is he really going to start his expedition from *here?* Manuel squeezed his eyes shut so he could believe it. Santa Barbara was a small mining town in 1597, the northernmost town in what was then New Spain.

Manuel didn't want to let Fernando know just how excited he was. After all, he was fourteen, and Fernando was only twelve. He had taken care of Fernando for five years now, so he should be...well dignified.

"I mean it, Manuel! I saw Don Juan's nephews riding fine horses and they had fancy saddles and a lot of men on horseback were riding with them and..."

"All right, all right, Fernando. I believe you. Just be quiet a minute and let me think."

Fernando straddled the crude bench under the hole in the wall they called a window, still breathing hard from his run up the hill. Manuel closed the door of the hut which had been home since the death of their father in a mining accident. Since then, Tia Margarita had let them live in the hut, built originally to store wood for the fireplace, back of her small house. Their mother had died when Fernando was born.

Tia Margarita was not really their aunt, but she allowed them several important privileges. One well-cooked meal a week. One bath a week in a tub by her fireplace. And sometimes an article of clothing. And sometimes she patched and mended what little clothing they had.

Manuel wondered if they were too young to go on the expedition. He had heard that no one under fifteen without their parents would be allowed, but both he and Fernando were large for their ages. The trouble was Manuel couldn't lie, and even if he could, Fernando's talk, talk, talk would give any secret away. Sometimes Manuel envied Fernando.

A *bleat-bleat* got his attention.

"Where's the corn for Captain-General Martinez?"

Fernando never forgot their goat. Except this time. A few minutes later he was on his way to the pen farther up the hill. Santa Barbara was all hills and dirt lanes.

Everyone talked about Captain-General Martinez, the goat who could do tricks. The two brothers led him down to the town's plaza every day where he stood on his hind legs like a dog. He even danced. They were trying to teach him to jump through a hoop. He was just about ready, Manuel thought. Then he would teach him to tap, tap, tap his foot to a count of

three. Then people would throw even more pennies!

With those pennies they bought food for the goat and themselves. They also earned a little money other ways, such as sweeping off the church steps.

For nearly a year now, they had heard about the great expedition of Don Juan de Oñate. He lived far from Santa Barbara in the silver-mining city of Zacatecas. He and his family were very wealthy. Don Juan had the title of Governor. If Manuel and Fernando could just go with him, who knew what riches they would discover? Everyone said there was gold and silver — more silver than in Santa Barbara's mines even — just for the taking. Maybe lying right out on the ground. And other jewels, too. Emeralds. Rubies.

They would no longer have to sweep steps. They would no longer be hungry. And neither would Captain-General Martinez. He could have a nice pen and a shed for the cold nights. And a woven blanket to lie on.

But Manuel didn't think of the riches so much as he thought of getting away from Santa Barbara, where every day he faced the threat of having to work in the mines. He and Fernando were getting big now and several mine owners noticed them in the plaza. Because the boys had dark eyes and hair, like their Indian grandfather, whom Manuel barely remembered, they stood the chance of being forced to work in the mines. Many Indians were.

Often, huddled on the floor of their hut, wrapped in rough blankets, they talked and dreamed into the night about getting away from Santa Barbara.

They wondered what they would see if they went with the Oñate expedition. Indians. Mountains. Gold. Bears. Lions. They couldn't stop thinking about all those things.

Even if the governor would let them join, what would they take? All they had was Captain-General Martinez and two old blankets.

How long would they be gone? Would they ever see the hills of Santa Barbara again? There weren't very many boys their age here, but still they would miss…yes, even Tia Margarita. But not the mine owners.

The next morning was Thursday. It was December, 1597, and the padre wanted the steps to the little church kept extra clean because Christmas was coming. In the afternoon, they would take Captain-General to the plaza. Maybe the governor's nephews would see him do his tricks.

At breakfast, Manuel heated tortillas over a fire outside while Fernando got milk from the farmer who lived nearby.

It's going to be a big day. And we'll actually see the beginnings of the expedition with our own eyes. Manuel remembered someone saying there would be several thousand animals — cows, horses, goats, donkeys. Others had talked about the governor's fine saddles, all trimmed in velvet. And his robes, trimmed with jewels.

As soon as they shared their breakfast with Captain-General Martinez, they rushed toward the plaza. Someone might be there who could tell them what was happening.

ALTHOUGH Manuel and Fernando often explored the hills of Santa Barbara, the memory of their father's accident kept them away from the mines. Manuel was only seven then, but the day was still clear in his mind. Tia Margarita rushed to the adobe house they shared with their father, grabbed them in her big arms and cried out the news. Many men, including her husband, died with their father. Manuel's nightmares that followed were always of mine disasters.

Life changed a lot for the boys after that, but at least they had one friend. Tia Margarita saw that they got food every day, and she often told them stories about their parents, who had been her friends. She also warned them against certain mine owners.

"You are orphans, so you better watch out they don't take you to the mines," she said.

Then, as more and more of her relatives came from Mexico City to live with her and work in the mines, she saw less and less of the boys. They had to learn a lot about taking care of themselves.

That was when they started sweeping the steps for the padre. He often gave them food or leather shoes made by the Indians who lived just outside the village.

It was one of the miners, Tia Margarita's brother-in-law, Señor Martinez, who gave them the baby goat. He said he was sorry it was not a nanny goat

so they could have milk, but Manuel and Fernando didn't care. In the miner's honor, they named him Captain-General Martinez, a title worthy of royalty.

"Why don't you kill him and eat him?"

At first, someone asked them that almost every day. Maybe that's why they started to train him, which everybody said couldn't be done. But they could, and did. After weeks and weeks, Captain-General Martinez started responding to their commands.

After people saw his tricks, few asked why they didn't use him for food. That was worth all the time it took, because they truly loved Captain-General Martinez. Still, they knew the cost of feeding themselves and the goat was very high. It was Tia Margarita who suggested they take him to the plaza. She even decorated a little basket and put in a penny herself in order, she said, to give people the right idea.

It worked beyond their dreams. Captain-General Martinez was the talk of the town.

The pennies didn't flow as well after a month or so because everyone had seen him perform. They thought of new tricks all the time, but it took weeks, even as smart as Captain-General Martinez was, to teach him to perform them well.

Last summer new people started coming into Santa Barbara almost every day. Now, in December, at least part of the expedition was here. Maybe even Don Juan de Oñate himself. Some said supplies were being stored just outside of town. Others said that only last week Don Juan's two nephews came to Santa Barbara. They didn't stop at the plaza, but everyone there stopped to watch them as they rode through the village.

They were brothers, too, Manuel was told. Juan and Vicente de Zaldivar. They were handsome as their horses, people said. Their saddles were trimmed in red velvet. Beside their horses trotted a long, lean dog with a spike collar.

Today the plaza was crowded with more people than Manuel and Fernando had ever seen. Cattle bawled from inside great clouds of dust. Horses whirled and turned as their riders took them this way and that. People yelled and sang. The noise was deafening.

All that day, they streamed through the town. Manuel and Fernando followed them until they suddenly remembered Captain-General Martinez! They hadn't fed him since early morning! He would jump over the fence and eat Tia Margarita's clothes!

By the time they returned to their hut they were out of breath and scared. But there was Captain-General Martinez, just as happy as could be. No piece of cloth hanging from his mouth. Nothing the matter at all. Manuel sighed in relief.

"What if we went on the expedition and Captain-General ate Don Juan's velvet robe?"

Fernando always seemed to ask the wrong questions at the wrong times. But Manuel was more worried about the mine owner he saw at the end of the street, just down the hill. He knew him by reputation, a mean hombre, in town to recruit workers. And Manuel thought he stared at the boys too long.

The next day more and more people, cows, sheep and horses came through Santa Barbara on their way to the camp outside of town. Manuel's head began to spin from all the noise, dust and confusion. Where is Fernando? Manuel whirled around to find him. Someone screamed. Horses and cows snorted and scrambled around him. *Where is Fernando?* He felt a sharp pain in his back and a stinging sensation in his neck. Then nothing.

"Manuel! Manuel! Wake up!"

Manuel opened his eyes to see Fernando leaning in his face.

"What happened?"

"You got kicked by a horse and this man picked you up."

Manuel's eyes slowly focused on a man's face.

"Are you alright, son? I don't think you're badly hurt.

"I'm Juan Zaldivar. What's your name?"

Slowly Manuel sat up and looked around him. Overhead he could see the blue sky through leaves of a tree. A horse grazed nearby.

"Thank you, sir. I guess I can get up now."

"Don't hurry. I'll help you home."

Manuel rode in front of him on the horse and Fernando walked behind. It was the first time Manuel had been on a horse. Along with the pain in his neck, Manuel felt a tingle of excitement.

"Tell me about yourself, Manuel. Where are your parents?"

Manuel ended the story of his parents just as they came to the bottom of the narrow street that led to their hut. He wondered if he should ask Señor Zaldivar in. He wanted to find out more about the expedition, too. Fernando solved the problem.

"Would you like to meet our goat?"

Fernando's question made Manuel feel hot all over. Now why would a man like Señor Zaldivar want to meet a goat? It was bad enough just to ask him inside their hut.

"You have a goat? I would like very much to meet him," Señor Zaldivar said.

Captain-General Martinez was on his best behavior. He stood on his hind legs, danced, and almost jumped through a hoop. Señor Zaldivar laughed and laughed. He laughed so hard that Manuel thought maybe now would be a good time to ask him about the expedition. He tried to think of just the right words.

"Señor Zaldivar, could we go with you on your expedition?" Fernando blurted out the question deep in Manuel's mind. He sighed, and waited for Señor Zaldivar to laugh even more.

Señor Zaldivar wiped the tears from his eyes.

"And the goat, too?"

"Yes, sir," Fernando said. "We couldn't leave Captain-General Martinez."

Señor Zaldivar stopped laughing. He looked first at Fernando, then at Manuel.

"You're serious, aren't you?"

Manuel nodded.

Señor Zaldivar brushed at his pants and began to leave.

"Tell you what. I'll come by tomorrow and take you out to the camp. You may not want to come when you see it. I must go now. I have a lot to do. Just be down at the plaza about noon tomorrow and I'll come by for you."

Manuel and Fernando followed him as he walked down the narrow street and got on his horse. For a long time, they watched as he disappeared past the plaza. It was quiet in the town now. Not even the mine owner was hanging around.

"Whee! Whee!" Fernando yelled, turning handsprings up the street toward the hut. For a moment Manuel was tempted to join him, then stopped as he felt the twinge in his neck. He was still a little dizzy, but he didn't know if it was from the accident or from thinking of what tomorrow might bring.

## 3

THEY TALKED for hours into the night. Thinking, planning, laughing, and wondering…what were they getting into?

Captain-General Martinez's hungry *bleat-bleat* wakened them. Long before noon they went to the plaza. The padre saw them from the church steps across the way and beckoned. Manuel felt bad, for they had not gone by yesterday, but how could they? The accident and all. Manuel explained, but the padre insisted on having the steps very, very clean…at this moment.

The dust and dirt on the steps was worse than ever from yesterday's crowd. To make matters worse, the wind was blowing. And the padre was cross. Still, they finished in time and rushed to the plaza. It was just noon. There were a few people sitting around, but no Señor Zaldivar.

"Should we go get Captain-General Martinez? New people are here."

Manuel would generally have agreed, but today…what if he came while they were gone?

"Let's wait awhile. If we had Captain-General we'd have to take him back to his pen if we went to the camp. Señor Zaldivar might not like that."

Fernando jumped over benches, made drawings in the dirt, whistled. Manuel leaned against a tree and kept his eyes on the road leading north. Everyone left the plaza. It was siesta time. Birds twittered sleepily in the trees. No Señor Zaldivar.

Darkness came. Manuel called Fernando, who by then was asleep, leaning against the water fountain.

"We have to take care of Captain-General," he said. "Besides, I'm hungry."

After supper, they fell asleep early, too disappointed to talk.

By morning, Manuel had made up his mind. He would no longer even think about the expedition. He and Fernando would just take Captain-General to the plaza and go on with life as usual. They could hide when the mine owners came to town. They could train the goat to do even more tricks. Someday they could earn enough money to go to Mexico City with him. There they could make a lot of money performing in the great plaza. Of course, it would take weeks and weeks to get there, maybe a year, as they would have to walk with their goat over 700 miles. He wondered how well he would do on such a long trip. It would be farther there than they would travel with the expedition. Of course, he didn't really know how far the expedition would go, but he had heard stories.

Down in the plaza, Captain-General Martinez delighted the crowds. People cheered and whistled and tossed many pennies into the basket. For a little while, Manuel didn't even think about Señor Zaldivar. That is, until the crowd suddenly quieted as two horsemen rode up. The two men tied their horses and walked toward Manuel and Fernando. One of them was Juan Zaldivar.

"Manuel and Fernando, this is my brother, Vicente. I have told him all about you. I couldn't come yesterday because we had to get ready for inspection. I'm sorry if I disappointed you."

The other Señor Zaldivar smiled and nodded to them as if they were grown-ups. Manuel like him immediately.

"Go on with the show."

Once again, Captain-General Martinez performed extremely well. The crowds laughed along with the Zaldivars. Manuel felt like laughing, too. But what was an inspection?

He wondered and wondered all through the performance.

Inspection, Señor Zaldivar explained later on their way to the camp, was required by the King of Spain. The Viceroy, who was appointed by the King to run Mexico, and the Royal Inspector, and their staff had to see if everything was in place for the expedition. They counted the people. They counted the horses and the cows, the sheep, oxen, hogs, goats, mules, tools, nails, shoes, clothing, medicine, and food.

As they neared the camp at the river, Manuel heard children yelling and cows bawling, men and women talking and laughing. A great roar went up to greet the two Zaldivars. One man called out, when he saw the goat, "He'll make a good roast come February!"

Manuel felt his heart in his throat. He had not wanted to bring Captain-General on this trip, but Señor Juan Zaldivar had insisted. The mere thought of killing Captain-General made his stomach feel funny. Señor Zaldivar grasped his arm.

"Now, don't worry. Nobody is going to eat your goat."

People were spread out under the trees as far as they could see. Cows and other animals were just beyond them. Fires were burning here and there and some people were cooking. The smell of roasted fish made Manuel's mouth water.

"Hungry?" Señor Zaldivar seemed able to read Manuel's mind.

"Yes, sir." It was Fernando who answered for both of them.

Juan Zaldivar led them toward a magnificent tent of bright colors. It was dark inside, but the smell of food took them to a table loaded with fruits, roasted fish and lamb, boiled corn, beans, squash, tortillas, nuts, and cakes. Señor Zaldivar just waved his hand toward it and left them to help themselves. Manuel had tied up Captain-General just outside. Without asking, Fernando quietly took an ear of corn to him. Manuel hoped no one saw him. Fernando seemed to have no such fears.

Señor Zaldivar returned in a few minutes.

"Come with me now, you two. You have to meet my uncle."

"You mean...Don Juan himself? Don Juan de Oñate?"

Señor Zaldivar smiled.

"That's right."

Manuel couldn't believe it. Here they were, two boys whose only possessions were a goat and two old blankets. And they were about to meet the great leader of a great expedition. And what then? Would the great leader smile and say yes, get ready, let's go?

Fernando slipped another ear of corn to Captain-General as they left the tent. Manuel quickly glanced at Señor Zaldivar to see if he approved. He didn't seem to mind.

Another tent, smaller but more elegant, sat behind Señor Zaldivar's. Inside, an older gentleman sat at a small table. He was writing something on a long piece of paper.

"So you want to go on the expedition, do you?"

The man spoke without even raising his eyes.

"Yes, your..." Manuel desperately searched his mind for the proper word.

"Highness," Fernando offered.

"Hmmph. I am not a highness. Just 'sir' is enough. I hear you have a trained goat. My nephew here, Juan, says he's pretty funny. Do you think you could keep people amused?"

"Oh, yes, sir," Manuel said. "We have done that many times."

"Good. That's the only reason I'll take you on, understand?"

Both boys answered. "Yes, sir."

Only then did Don Juan lay his pen aside and look at the two boys.

"You have a name for this goat?"

Before Manuel or Fernando could answer, Señor Zaldivar started laughing.

"What's so funny?" Don Juan asked grumpily. "I just asked his name."

"That's what's so funny. His name is the same as your title — Captain-General."

Juan Zaldivar howled with laughter again. Don Juan looked serious for awhile, then he too smiled, and joined in the laughter.

Finally, he stopped, but not before Manuel and Fernando were thoroughly miserable.

"Oh, don't mind us, boys. We have so little to laugh about these days that your goat is really welcome."

"Just keep Captain-General out of the way until I call him," Don Juan said. "I don't want any trouble from him, or he'll be goat stew."

As they left, Manuel shuddered, for he knew he meant what he said. He looked for Fernando, but he had disappeared into the other tent. Manuel

guessed why. Another ear of corn for Captain-General Martinez. *That* was a good way to get into trouble.

Back again at their hut, Manuel and Fernando tried to think what they would tell Tia Margarita. Maybe she would be glad to see them go, Manuel thought.

Manuel was wrong. Tia Margarita burst into tears and held the boys tight in her arms.

"Oh, you poor children. You'll never come back. Or if you do you'll be grown up. And what about those strange people up north? I hear they…"

"Cut you up in little pieces?"

Oh, Fernando, Manuel thought. You always seem to know just what to say.

Tia Margarita burst into a fresh set of tears and howls.

"Fernando," Manuel said. "You should be ashamed."

"I'm not scared or anything," Fernando said. "I just heard that's what they do."

"Well, you don't need to talk about it."

Tia Margarita dried her tears.

"I have a present for you. I was saving it for Christmas, but since you're leaving before then, I'll get it."

Pretty soon she was back from the only other room in the house with something in her hands.

It was new shirts and pants for them both.

Manuel felt tears rush to his eyes. Fernando hugged her tightly.

"Oh, thank you, Tia Margarita. We'll always remember you. And someday we may be back, and we'll be very rich and you can live with us in a fine house," Manuel promised.

That just caused Tia Margarita to cry more.

EARLY THE NEXT morning even before Tia Margarita stirred, the boys and Captain-General Martinez were on their way. Down the hill, through the plaza, and on toward the camp to the north. Señor Zaldivar had told them they should be there by mid-afternoon. The Viceroy and Royal Inspector were expected the next day. Manuel and Fernando would put Captain-General Martinez through his paces just for their amusement. Señor Zaldivar thought it would make a good impression.

The goat certainly made an impression all right. After his first performance, with Don Juan de Oñate, his two nephews, and the two important gentlemen from Mexico City looking on, Captain-General went over to the Viceroy and took off the velvet hat from his head. Before Manuel could stop him, he was chewing it as if it were an ear of corn.

The Viceroy quickly pulled his sword from his scabbard and looked as if he would bring it down on Captain-General's head. Juan Zaldivar stopped him.

"Sir, please. We will serve you goat stew later, after my uncle gives you one of his finest hats."

Manuel took one look at the Viceroy and an angry Don Juan de Oñate, grabbed Captain-General's rope, pulled at Fernando and ran. But Señor Zaldivar came after them.

"Here, now, boys. Don't let such a little incident chase you away. Everybody laughed about it afterwards."

Manuel found it hard to believe him.

"But he wants to eat our goat…"

"Never! I told him Captain-General Martinez was too tough, that we had much better ones to eat."

"But—"

"No buts. Please come back. We all need you and your goat to make us laugh. Please."

Fernando looked at Manuel. Manuel looked at Fernando. Fernando looked at the ground.

"What do you say, Fernando?"

"I don't want them to eat Captain-General Martinez," he said. A tear dropped to the ground.

"Neither do I," Manuel said. Then he turned to Señor Zaldivar.

"Do we always have to be scared somebody will eat him?"

Señor Zaldivar frowned and put an arm across Manuel's shoulder.

"I'll be honest. I think somebody will be thinking that all the time. All I can promise you is that I will do everything in my power to keep that from happening. I promise you."

Manuel looked at Fernando again, then up at Señor Zaldivar.

"I believe you."

But Manuel didn't know if it was because he really did or because he wanted to believe him.

"I won't say it's up to you, Fernando. I know it's up to both of us, but if you say yes, I'll say yes, and if you say no, I'll say no."

Fernando waited a long time before he answered, his dark eyes serious.

"I say yes."

Señor Zaldivar smiled and slapped them on their backs.

"Good! Now, I'll tell you my plan in the morning. First, I'll find you a good spot for camping. I'll get you some food, too."

Señor Zaldivar took them to the edge of the camp.

"Tomorrow a lot more people and animals will be here. It will take a few weeks before we can travel. In the meantime, just learn to live out in the open. Keep yourselves and your clothes clean in that river there. Someone will bring you food."

It was just as he said. Every day, a horseman came by and dropped a bag of food for them. They watched other people cook over their open fires and learned from them how to live outdoors. After awhile, they felt like old-timers. They made a few friends, too, but many of them kept making remarks about eating the goat. When that happened, they moved a little farther down the line of campers. Not too far, or the horseman with the food might miss them.

Days passed, but finally a morning came when they heard a lot of people yelling at their horses and cows. They knew the time had come to begin the great expedition.

It was January. At Santa Barbara's high elevation, nights were quite cold. By mid morning, however, the sun warmed the air.

Manuel and Fernando gathered their few belongings, including the new shirts and pants Tia Margarita had given them. They also had new leather shoes, given them by the padre. They had already washed their blankets. Manuel wondered what lay ahead. Sometimes he worried.

He worried more after Señor Zaldivar came that morning. Instead of laughing when he saw Captain-General Martinez, he frowned and looked very serious.

"Is something wrong?" Fernando asked. It was a question Manuel had wanted to ask.

"I don't know. My uncle has decided not to follow the way all the other explorers have gone. Instead, he will make a direct line away from the river and go straight north."

Señor Zaldivar drew a map in the sand.

"You see, instead of following the Conchos River to the Rio Grande, and then following the Rio Grande toward this range of mountains, we go straight across here."

"That's good. It's shorter, isn't it, sir?" Manuel asked.

"Indeed it is. It's weeks and weeks shorter, but...."

He stood up then and wandered off, a worried look on his face. He turned back and placed his hands on Manuel's shoulders.

"It also may be very dangerous. No one has ever gone that way before. There may be no water. Food may be very scarce. There may be Indians more fierce than we have ever seen. I'm not sure such young fellows like you should be going. Maybe you would be better off working in the mines."

"Oh-h-h," Fernando wailed.

"Ssh, Fernando. We must listen."

"You're very wise, Manuel, so you must make this decision yourself, and Fernando, listen to your brother."

"Yes, sir," Fernando replied meekly, for once.

Manuel squatted on the ground, looking at the map. He was as disappointed as Fernando, but he was responsible for him, too.

"What about Captain-General Martinez?" Manuel dreaded to hear the answer.

"Well," Señor Zaldivar said. "You know, of course, that if worse comes to worst and people are hungry, they will eat him just as they'll eat all the other goats. But he makes people laugh and they certainly need to laugh. Most likely he would be the last goat to go."

Manuel had never heard anyone say that people needed to laugh. Still, he remembered the many times the goat had made the people laugh at the plaza. And how they had thanked him and Fernando. Maybe laughing really was good for you. He wished he could laugh now.

Señor Zaldivar started to mount his horse.

"Before you decide, think it over tonight. I'll be back in the morning to get your answer."

By dawn, Manuel and Fernando had reached a decision. As promised, Señor Zaldivar came riding up amid all the confusion of campers getting ready to leave.

"Well, let's hear it," he said, slipping off his horse easily and expertly.

"We've decided to..."

"Go," Fernando interrupted.

Señor Zaldivar looked at Manuel.

"Sure?"

"Yes, sir. We talked about it a lot, all night. We decided we could learn to live just as the others have. We're young and strong. And we, well, we want to go..."

Señor Zaldivar seemed happy at their decision.

"Well, both of you come back with me now to my tent. One of you can ride with me on the horse and we'll lead Captain-General Martinez."

"Is the Viceroy still there?" Manuel was afraid their goat would not survive another meeting with this royal man who wanted to make him into goat stew.

"He's leaving. We probably won't even see him. And if we do, I'll say this is a twin goat. That we used the other one for stew."

"Señor Zaldivar, that's lying," Fernando said.

"Fernando! What are you saying?"

"He's right, Manuel. We should all be so honest. I promise you we won't even see him."

That morning, Captain-General Martinez performed before the great Don Juan de Oñate and his fellow officers. They laughed and applauded and said "bravo, bravo" a lot. Fernando beamed, and Manuel was very happy.

Don Juan said the goat and the two boys would be a fine addition for the long trip north.

"But," he added, "if you want to protect that goat, you'd better stay at the end of the line. Otherwise he'll get mixed up with all the others and…well…."

Manuel knew exactly what he meant.

SEÑOR ZALDIVAR took them back to their campsite, and as he went, he talked to them about surviving the desert.

"I'll tell you what an old Indian told me," he began.

"There are several things to remember about water. First, you can live without food longer than you can without water.

"This means you have to know how to find it. Remember first that water runs downhill, so you might find it at the bottom of cliffs or mountains. Birds and other animals have to have water, too. Watch where they fly in the early morning or just before dark. Plants, too, need water to live. Where they are greenest, there is water. Plants also store water. Prickly pear cactus will give you both food and water. And so will a lot of other plants."

Señor Zaldivar told them many things about surviving in the desert. At times, Manuel grew frightened at all the possibilities. Señor Zaldivar told them not to worry.

"You may never need to know all these things. But a little knowledge won't hurt you."

As he started to leave, he handed each a knife in a leather sheath.

"Be very careful with them. They will help you do everything from building a fire to making clothes," he said, and was gone.

Manuel and Fernando looked at the knives, comparing them with each other's. Manuel's had a black handle. Fernando's was brown. Both were very sharp.

Señor Zaldivar told Manuel and Fernando to wait by the side of the trail until everyone had passed. They would know the procession was ended when his brother, Vicente, came by. They were not to be surprised if it took all day.

It did take all day and into the night. The dust from 400 people, 7,000 cows, horses, sheep, and goats covered them from head to foot. The noise was deafening. When Vicente Zaldivar finally appeared, he told them that all the people and animals made a line at least four miles long. He told them something else.

"We'll be very lucky to cover more than five miles a day," he said.

Manuel didn't know how far it was to where they were going, but he knew it must be a long distance. And at five miles a day, the days might turn into weeks and months. Were they doing the right thing?

Grimy and dirty, they found a place by the river and bathed. The water was icy cold. By morning, however, they were in line, ready to go on their great adventure.

There were times in the next two weeks when they were almost too tired to keep up. Just ahead of them was a family of six, Señor and Señora Moreno and four tiny children, Maria, Lupe, Berta, and Luis. As they became acquainted, Manuel and Fernando took Luis, the youngest, for rides on Captain-General Martinez. Often the Morenos asked them to share their food. In exchange, the boys took care of the children.

There were many delays. They camped for what seemed like weeks near a river, but in early February, 1598, they started through the desert.

This was not a desert of sand. The Chihuahuan Desert has some sand dunes, but it is mostly bushes and cactus. It is very dry. People traveling through it must know how to find water, particularly during the spring when the winds blow and days vary from very hot to cold.

The Morenos had one cow, a two-wheeled cart, and an ox to pull it. They carried the children, clothes, food and cooking pots in the cart. On hot days, the Morenos invited Manuel and Fernando to place their blankets and extra clothes in the cart. This made it possible for Manuel and Fernando to wander away from the line to hunt for food and water.

It was Captain-General Martinez who discovered the best way to hunt rabbits for food. When a coyote captured one, Captain-General Martinez frightened it away from the dead rabbit before it was eaten. When the story was told to others in the line, they could not believe it.

"How can a goat scare a coyote?" they asked. "Coyotes eat goats!"

The truth was that all Captain-General Martinez had to do was to stand on his hind legs and *bleat-bleat*, and the coyote ran away.

But water was harder to find. The Morenos carried several pots of water on the wagon. They stored the water they found at springs along the way, and even though they could carry very little, they often shared with Manuel and Fernando.

One day they found no springs.

"I'm sorry, boys," Señor Moreno said. "We will all have to find water for ourselves. No one told us this would happen."

"Maybe Fernando and I can find water for all of us. We'll go look if you will keep Captain-General Martinez."

Señor Moreno agreed. Manuel could tell by looking at his face that he did not believe they could find water. Manuel didn't believe it either. All he knew was that he had to try very hard.

First, Manuel tried to remember just what Señor Zaldivar had said. "Look around you. If you see hills, remember that water flows downstream. You may find it at the bottom."

Manuel looked, but he saw no hills.

"Watch for birds early in the mornings or late in the evenings. They will fly toward water."

Manuel saw no birds. Perhaps it was too late in the morning.

"Look for dry stream beds. Where it bends, you can often find water if you dig."

The only dry stream bed Manuel had seen was one they crossed more than a week ago.

"Look for reeds, grass, willows, cottonwoods. These plants grow near water."

Manuel saw only dry looking cactus plants. Cactus! Of course! Even at home in Santa Barbara, they often scraped off the sharp spines and sucked on the moist cactus pads. Often they roasted them for food. The fire burned off the spines.

"It's not the best substitute for water," he told Señor Moreno, "but it will help."

Señor Moreno smiled gratefully and took the cactus pads.

"We'll keep looking for signs of water," Manuel told him. Before he could continue his search, however, Juan Zaldivar rode up on his horse. He seemed glad to see them.

"It is time for you to make us laugh," he said. "People are not very happy going through this dry desert."

All day for two days, Manuel and Fernando took Captain-General Martinez up the line. And people did laugh. When Fernando told them of how the goat found food for them, they cheered. No one mentioned goat stew.

On the second day, they performed for Don Juan de Oñate and his family and fellow officers at the front of the line. Again, they cried "bravo, bravo," and asked for more tricks.

Manuel and Fernando had been too busy looking for food and water to try training him in new tricks. They knew they would have to start soon, for the goat was the only reason Don Juan had let them come.

6

THERE WERE other problems that kept Manuel and Fernando from taking the time to train Captain-General Martinez. The first problem today was a rattlesnake coiled on the path in front of them, just behind the Moreno family. Fernando sucked in his breath, but before he could open his mouth to yell, Manuel grabbed him by his shirt from behind.

"Don't move," he told Fernando in a whisper. "Don't even breathe."

Oblivious to the danger, Captain-General Martinez munched on a bush some distance away. If he saw the snake, who knew what would happen, Manuel thought. All he knew now was that they must remain still. Señor Zaldivar had warned them about snakes and how important it was not to disturb them.

And he was right. Pretty soon, the rattler slithered off into the bush. Fernando heaved a sigh of relief and called Captain-General Martinez to return to the path.

They walked through thickets of brush that tore at their clothes. They learned to stay away from cholla cactus. The rocks and sand bruised their feet, especially through the valleys between hills. The new leather shoes the padre had given them when they left Santa Barbara had worn out completely.

"You're pretty smart boys," Señor Zaldivar told them when he saw their bare feet. "Did you ever wonder how the Indian made those shoes that you've been wearing?"

"Yes," Manuel said, as if he had just had a great revelation. "They were made from leather. We can do that."

Fernando did not appear enthusiastic, but he joined Manuel and Captain-General Martinez the next morning before the march began in search of an animal whose hide they could make into shoes. But they did not have to use the goat's powers to frighten away an animal from its freshly killed prey. They found one dead and already eaten except for its hide. It was a bobcat.

As Señor Zaldivar had told them, they laid the skin flat, scraped it with the knives he had given them, and dragged it back to their accustomed place in the line behind the Morenos. But the line was already moving ahead. In order to make shoes from the bobcat's hide they had to remove the fur first. And to do that they had to keep the hide in shade and in the dirt for two or three days so they could get the fur off.

What to do? Could they catch up with the line if they stayed behind? Could they walk at all without the shoes?

Manuel looked at the painful bruises on his feet and on Fernando's. He knew that the answer to their problems was risky, but they had to take that risk. Maybe it wasn't all that great a risk since Señor Zaldivar came from time to time to check up on them. Still, sometimes two weeks went by without their seeing him.

"Ow-w-w," Fernando moaned, rubbing his feet. Captain-General Martinez answered with a *bleat-bleat* and went on munching. It seemed he never quit.

With a sinking feeling in the pit of his stomach, Manuel watched the line move without them. He stood watching it a long time before he began to cover the hide with sand.

Not far away was a dry stream bed where he might find water. Dig where the stream bed bends, Señor Zaldivar had told them. He hoped a bend was nearby, because he knew he couldn't walk on his sore feet very far. If necessary, they could slice off the top of the barrel cactus near where they had found the bobcat. But the juice was bitter. Maybe they could find other water-storing plants, too.

Fortunately, Manuel told Fernando, they had enough food to last a day or so. A little dried beef, corn, and tortillas, and maybe they could find wild grapes. They would build a fire to keep away animals and heat their food. More importantly, they could stick their feet out from under their blankets toward the fire to stop the hurting.

The night was clear. Manuel studied the stars dashing in and out of dark doorways overhead. Fernando was already sound asleep. Captain-General Martinez lay beside them, gently wheezing. He had kept them warm many nights since they had joined the expedition.

What an adventure this has been, Manuel thought. Tia Margarita seemed far away, but at times he could almost feel her big arms around him. His stomach growled at the thought of her good meals. Still, he had learned much, and every time he learned something new, he felt good. As if he were like Don Juan de Oñate. Only not as rich.

When the sun warmed their faces the next morning, they began their search for water. Limping carefully through the brush, they came to the stream bed. To their left, upstream, Manuel noticed a hill. Not a very high one, but he began also to see small green trees and, yes, there were some birds. Exactly what Señor Zaldivar had told them. Over there, in that place, the stream bed made a sharp turn. Just below the turn, they found a small puddle of water.

"Let's dig," Manuel told Fernando. With their bare hands they dug as fast as they could and were soon rewarded. The farther they dug, the more water seeped into the hole. It did not take long for them to have enough to quench their thirst. But they had no container with them, so Fernando went back to the campsite to get the one pot they had kept for the purpose. Captain-General Martinez went with him.

Alone, Manuel kept digging. A slight sound he couldn't recognize caused him to stop. As he had learned from the encounter with the rattlesnake, he kept perfectly still. It had to be an animal's sound, but what animal?

A buzzing insect swept around his head. He resisted the urge to slap at it. Ever so slowly he turned his head toward the sound and was horrified to see two coyotes looking at him.

They were not twenty feet away. Manuel froze with fear, but all sorts of thoughts crowded his brain. If he were killed, what would happen to Fernando? And to his beloved goat?

And then Manuel heard another sound that frightened him even more. The *bleat-bleat* of the goat. Could he warn his brother without turning the coyotes' attention to him and the goat?

Fernando was whistling. How could he whistle at a time like this? Manuel knew that was a silly thought. Fernando didn't even know about the coyotes.

But suddenly, Manuel knew that Fernando did know about the coyotes.

7

FERNANDO'S SCREAM echoed through the small canyon. Manuel's eyes were glued to the two coyotes, who drew back a short distance, then turned as if to attack the goat and Fernando. But then something happened that would forever remain in Manuel's memory and no doubt in Fernando's. Captain-General Martinez started toward the coyotes, then stopped, reared back on his hind legs and let out the loudest *bleat-bleat* the boys had ever heard.

The startled coyotes turned and, with their tails beneath their legs, ran off into the underbrush.

"Manuel! Manuel! Did you see that?"

The impossible just happened. A goat had frightened not one, but two killer-coyotes. No one would ever believe this story, Manuel thought, thinking of how much Señor Zaldivar would enjoy the story even if he didn't believe it. If Manuel hadn't seen it, he wouldn't believe it either.

Hungry coyotes nearby were a real threat. How could they protect themselves at night when they were asleep? They couldn't walk far enough to reach safety. They simply had to stay here. Near their food and near the hide for their shoes. What could they do?

Captain-General Martinez provided the answer.

The low bushes that surrounded them included the treacherous cholla cactus, with its thick and light needles. The merest touch can detach millions of them onto the skin. Manuel and Fernando learned weeks ago how bad they

were. Apparently, Captain-General Martinez had not. In his constant search for something to munch, he touched his moist nose against the cactus. He backed off so fast and in such pain that he would have run in panic had Fernando not grabbed him around the neck.

"Hey, it's all right. Take it easy. We'll get the stickers out," Fernando soothed him.

They spent hours removing the tiny hooked spines from the goat's nose. It was very difficult because, if they were not careful, they would have the spines in their own fingers. Captain-General Martinez patiently allowed them to work. As they worked, they talked about how they could protect themselves when night fell. When they were with the others in the great long line, there was so much noise, so many campfires, and so many people, that they slept on the ground curled up in their blankets without the slightest fear.

Here, however, no one was around except the animals. And who knew what animals?

"We might find a cave over there in that hill," Fernando offered.

"With our feet?"

"Well, maybe we could dig a cave in the side right over there."

Fernando pointed to an embankment across the dry stream bed, near where they had found water.

"I think I have a better idea. As soon as we get Captain-General's stickers removed, I'll show you. It just might work. Captain-General gave me the idea. Notice how he backed off from that cactus?"

When the final sticker was removed, Manuel got his knife and started cutting large branches of sage brush and mesquite, and stuck the thick ends into the ground in a 'U'. He directed Fernando to cut as many branches as he could. Manuel then extended branches over the closed end of the U until he had a shelter big enough for himself, Fernando and Captain-General Martinez. Just outside the open end, Manuel and Fernando gathered enough other branches to use as a "front door."

If a little cactus could keep Captain-General Martinez away, then thick layers of brush ought to keep out animals during the night, Manuel thought. And during their sleep that night when Manuel heard something sniffing around, he knew he was right.

Two very hot days passed during which they were grateful for the shade their new "house" provided. As the sun started to go down toward the end of the second day, Manuel dug up the hide for their shoes. The fur came off easily, and the leather was soft and easy to bend.

Following the pattern of their old shoes as best they could, they soon had protection for their feet. What they didn't use of the hide for their shoes, they rolled tightly and tied around Captain-General's neck to carry. At first he wanted to eat it, but then apparently decided it was not worth the trouble.

They traveled the next morning for only a few hours until it was so hot they could walk no longer. They had no fear of losing the expedition, because, of course, so many people and animals left a trail easy to follow. Still, Manuel wondered if they would catch them before they reached the great river of the north.

They found a small bit of shade on one side of a big yucca plant and stopped until late afternoon.

A little farther on, Fernando found a rock outcropping with several water holes. They drank thirstily. They used one waterhole for cooking what few beans they had left. By heating small rocks on top of a campfire and then scooping up the rocks with a flat stone and dropping them into the water hole, they had boiling water. Perfect for the beans.

No sooner had they eaten the beans than a dark cloud appeared overhead. A big clap of thunder sent them flying toward one of the large rock over-hangs where they found shelter from the brief rainstorm. It was as if the cloud knew they needed the water holes replenished.

"Let's stay here for the night," Manuel suggested.

"Fine by me."

Captain-General Martinez bleated as if to agree.

"We need hats," Manuel said. "I think we can make them with yucca leaves, but we'll have to soften them so we won't get cut. Those leaves are as sharp as our knives."

"How about boiling them first in one of the water holes?"

Even as he spoke, he was using his knife to cut some of the leaves from a nearby yucca. The snowy white blossoms produced banana-like fruit that was delicious. The flowers and seeds of the ocotillo were also tasty. Señor Zaldivar had told them they could make a wonderful drink by soaking the blossoms in water.

By night they gathered enough desert food for a meal that, while it did not resemble Tia Margarita's cooking, was tasty and filling.

Afterward, they took the softened yucca leaves and wove them into what could pass for hats. They were proud of them and of their new, if somewhat too large, shoes. They cut thin straps from some of the remaining hide to tie their shoes on firmly.

When morning came they were ready to try to catch the expedition.

THEY COULD no longer see the small cloud of dust from the other travelers. The land stretched out before them endlessly. From time to time they heard the twittering of birds or the buzz of insects, but otherwise it was quiet. Manuel stopped to look behind them to make sure no animal had followed. He had that eerie feeling someone or something was watching them.

By mid-afternoon, however, he had lost the feeling and was pleased when he saw a small cloud of dust far, far ahead. That would be the expedition.

It was not the expedition. It was a dust storm the likes of which they had never seen. Their first inkling of what was happening was a wind that whipped their new hats from their heads and sent them sailing into the sky.

Then the dust came in great rolling clouds of brown. They could not see or speak. They could barely hear Captain-General Martinez's *bleat-bleat*. They had no shelter. If any had been near they could not have seen it. All they could do was sit down with their backs to the wind and cling to each other until it blew over. They waited for what seemed hours, but finally the wind settled into a light breeze.

Manuel worried about the time they had lost, but surely, he told Fernando, they could catch up tomorrow. Now, however, they had to find shelter for the night. Quickly they made another shelter of shrub cuttings. Manuel wondered how far south the wind had blown their other one. He hoped the wind would not blow tonight.

For water and food, they found prickly pear cactus pads which they de-thorned in their small campfire. Captain-General Martinez scared away an eagle from its freshly killed rabbit which Manuel skinned and roasted. It was not, he thought, a bad evening, but he still had that funny feeling.

"Have you seen anything following us?"

Fernando's eyes grew large.

"No. Is something following us?"

Manuel was sorry he had frightened Fernando, and dismissed his question with a grin.

"Just kidding," he said.

"Thanks, Manuel. Thanks a lot."

In spite of Manuel's uneasiness, he, Fernando, and even the goat slept throughout the night.

The same feeling of being watched haunted Manuel throughout the next day, but he could neither hear nor see anything. Toward dusk, however, he forgot about it, for he could clearly see the dust from the expedition. This time he knew that it was no dust storm. Tomorrow, surely, they would be able to catch up with them. Their spirits were high as they again made a house from shrubs.

By noon the next day, they could almost make out people and horses in the far distance. In spite of the heat, they ran.

"Manuel! Fernando!"

It was Señor Zaldivar on horseback! The sight of him was a happy moment. He slid from his horse and shook their hands, seemingly as happy as they were. He walked along with them a short distance as Manuel and Fernando told him of their adventures, especially the time Captain-General Martinez saved their lives.

"You two up here on the horse. I'll run beside you and we'll catch up in no time," he directed.

All the Morenos greeted the boys warmly. Señora Moreno told them how worried she had been.

"Luis missed you most of all," she said. And as if to prove her right, the little toddler ran to Manuel and hugged his legs. Manuel picked him up and swung him over his head. This was like having a family, he thought.

Señor Zaldivar told them the line was not moving for about three days so everyone could rest and that he would be back to get them in two days.

"I want you to tell the story of how Captain-General Martinez saved you from the coyotes," he said.

"Hah," Fernando hooted. "He won't believe us."

"Don't be too sure of that," Señor Zaldivar said as he mounted his horse and galloped off.

Señor and Señora Moreno insisted the boys eat with them that night. The food, mostly corn, beans, squash and wild grapes, was a huge treat after the desert food the boys had been eating. Manuel knew the Morenos didn't have a lot of food to spare, so he doubly appreciated their invitation.

Two days later, the boys were rested, and Captain-General Martinez was in great spirits. Señor Zaldivar came for them, as promised, and the goat entertained everyone up and down the line.

"I think it's time you present yourselves again to my uncle," Señor Zaldivar said.

Manuel looked at Fernando, who had that look of dread in his eyes every time Don Juan's name came up.

"Yes, sir," Manuel said.

Don Juan seemed pleased to see them, however, and told them of his plans.

"Tomorrow, some of our people will scout the road ahead of us. We'll wait here until they send back a messenger, so we will want you to entertain us again," Don Juan said. He seemed to be examining them very carefully.

Manuel was suddenly very conscious of his and Fernando's worn clothes and over-sized, crudely made shoes. Their recent adventures had worn out even the fine pants and shirts that Tia Margarita gave them so very long ago. As if he had read Manuel's mind, Don Juan reached out and felt the ragged sleeve of his shirt.

"Juan. Get my trunk brought in here. I think I have some things that will fit these boys. They're pretty good size fellows."

When two soldiers brought the magnificent trunk in, Don Juan directed them to open it and spread out the contents. Manuel had never seen such finery. A blue velvet cloak was trimmed in jewels. There was a red one, too. And hats with feathers, velvet caps just like the one Captain-General had taken from the Viceroy's head, Manuel remembered. He reached out to touch the beautiful clothes, then quickly drew back his hand.

Don Juan lifted one layer of the clothes and found pants and shirts made of sturdy material, and handed them to the boys.

"Go over there and try these on. They might be a little big, but they'll do."

The clothes were a little large, but Manuel didn't care. Fernando grinned happily.

"Well, how's that, boys? Think those will suit you for a few weeks?"

"Yes, sir," Manuel answered. "We thank you very much."

Don Juan was much kinder than before. But suddenly, his face turned red and he roared.

"That goat! What is he doing?"

In horror, Manuel turned behind him in time to see that Captain-General had munched halfway through the magnificent blue velvet cloak.

9

"THAT'S IT! This goat has to go. Juan, take it to the back for slaughter. At once!"

Manuel tried to remember later what he had done. When he heard Don Juan de Oñate pronounce this sentence, whatever it was, he knew he had left the timid Manuel behind him, and that he would never be the same boy again. Fernando told him that everyone stepped back as Manuel defiantly took the goat and then shook his fist at Don Juan.

"No, sir. You will not take our goat. We will leave the expedition right now, but no, sir, you will not take Captain-General Martinez."

With that, Manuel pulled Captain-General along with him and took Fernando by the arm. All three marched out of the tent past astonished soldiers and other onlookers. Don Juan's mouth was open in amazement. Who had ever — other than the Viceroy — questioned Don Juan's authority?

Halfway down the line, past all the curious travelers, Manuel suddenly stopped and looked down at his new clothes.

"We have to take these back and get our old clothes," he told Fernando.

"With Captain-General Martinez? They'll kill him."

"You take Captain-General to the end of the line and wait for me. I'll take mine back now and change and get your clothes. You can send these new ones back by one of the Morenos. Just don't let Captain-General out of your sight.

With that, Manuel turned back toward the governor's tent. His anger made his stride long and fast. But soon his anger was gone. In its place, he felt a new sensation. Of being his own self. And he knew, then, that he was in charge of his life.

This he had learned from his entire life before this moment, from the deaths of his parents, from life in Santa Barbara, and now from the long journey and the hardships in the desert. He had earned his own dignity. And Don Juan de Oñate, no matter how great he was, could never change that.

No one was near the tent, and Manuel's and Fernando's old clothes were in plain sight. Quickly, Manuel stripped the new shirt and pants off and slipped into his old ragged clothes.

By running hard, he was soon back at the end of the line where Fernando waited with the goat.

"We have to hide," Manuel told Fernando. "Give the new clothes to the Morenos and ask them to give them to Señor Zaldivar to return to his uncle."

Without saying goodbye to anyone, Manuel and Fernando slipped away

with Captain-General Martinez. It was nearing sundown, so they knew they had to find shelter for the night in a hurry. There was no time to build a bush house, as Fernando called it. They headed for a nearby outcropping of rocks and found a ledge to sleep under.

But Manuel didn't sleep much. He kept thinking of what he had done. They could all be punished severely. And Captain-General would be goat stew, for sure.

As the stars came out and the soft noises of night arose, Manuel again had that feeling of being watched. The loud snap of a twig made him sit up suddenly and crack his head on the rock overhang. He muffled a cry of pain, settled back, and just listened. He heard no more and toward morning sank into a deep sleep of exhaustion.

Just as the early morning sun was slipping over their rocky shelter, Manuel opened his eyes to a semi-circle of six Indian men with spears, all looking at the boys and the goat. Heart in his mouth, he nudged Fernando. Fernando let out a yelp and edged behind Captain-General Martinez.

The goat, who had also slept soundly from exhaustion, awakened with a *bleat-bleat*. Manuel thought perhaps if he could get him to a place where he could stand without falling off the ledge, he might frighten them away as he had the coyotes. Slowly, he edged to a spot clear of any rock overhang, and directed Captain-General to stand on his hind legs and *bleat-bleat*.

When the goat did so, the Indian men merely laughed and pointed. They seemed to enjoy the sight as much as the travelers on the expedition had. Manuel tried to control his trembling. Fernando was about to squeeze into the rock itself. Still, the Indians just stood and watched them, laughing and gesturing.

Broad smiles lined their faces, and they began to gesture for the boys to follow them. One of them, who seemed to be a leader, said "no hurt, no hurt."

Manuel stretched out his hand to Fernando, who was still clinging to Captain-General Martinez. Slowly, the two boys and the goat went forward to the Indians, who then turned and started back up the trail toward the expedition. They continued beckoning.

When Manuel turned around, as if to go in the other direction, three of the Indians ran and blocked him. Should he risk his and Fernando's life by turning back to Santa Barbara, or should they return to the expedition and take their chances? In Manuel's new feeling about himself, it seemed sensible to take their chances with the Indians.

They would probably soon know the answer, Manuel thought, because he could see in the distance the familiar man on horseback, Señor Zaldivar. Well, at least it wasn't Don Juan.

"You gave us a scare, Manuel," Señor Zaldivar said. "We thought we had lost you."

"Señor Zaldivar, you have been very kind to us, but your uncle is determined to kill Captain-General Martinez, and that's why we have to leave the expedition."

"No, he isn't. I've just told him how Captain-General Martinez saved your lives, and I asked him to promise never to threaten him again."

"Oh, he wouldn't believe that story. Nobody would," Manuel said.

"Oh, yes, he believes it all right. Our friends have verified the story." He waved a hand toward the six smiling Indians.

"Them? How could they know anything about it?"

"Because, when you stayed behind to make your shoes, and when I told Don Juan about it, he sent his friends to watch after you. They were with you all the time."

"So that's why I had that funny feeling someone was watching us," Manuel said.

Señor Zaldivar just smiled.

"Come back to us. We'll soon be to the great river."

## 10

IN THE DAYS that followed, horses became so thirsty they were half blind. Shoes wore out. Wind blew constantly. Dust caked around Manuel's and Fernando's eyes and mouths. They scouted the countryside for cactus pads and the bitter barrel cactus. Even that seemed dry. For seven days they traveled without seeing a single spring or water hole. It seemed they traveled by inches instead of miles.

Then late one afternoon, a huge black cloud moved rapidly toward them, and rain fell for at least half an hour, so hard it seemed they might drown standing up.

Everyone called it a miracle. They filled what containers they could find, and then drank thirstily.

Had it not been for the rain, Manuel felt no one would have been able to go on. Now, however, everyone was in good spirits and moved forward rapidly. At one place they had to cross giant, snowy white sand dunes, through which horses had a hard time walking. Captain-General Martinez fairly pranced across them.

Again, the heat rose, and water became scarce. One morning, Manuel noticed a flock of birds overhead. They were going in the same direction the travelers were. Could it mean water?

That day, Señor Zaldivar came to ask them to entertain the travelers once more.

"I think we are only a few days away from the river, and everyone must make a large effort. All the travelers, and even the cattle, are footsore and weary. If we don't do something to help, we'll never make it," Señor Zaldivar said.

Captain-General Martinez was magnificent. He pranced, and even leaped through a hoop that Fernando held for him. As tired as the travelers were, they cheered for every trick he performed.

It was well they had some encouragement, for two days more of hunger and thirst were all but unbearable. Manuel saw more birds then, and in the distance he thought he could make out trees. Trees! How he longed to lie under the shade of one.

And then, there it was, the great river, the Río del Norte. They heard it first. The sound of splashing and shouting was from those who had already reached it. Cottonwood trees, salt cedar, and tornillo bush lined the banks. Hundreds were swimming. Children were laughing and playing. Others were fishing or roasting ducks and geese on a great bonfire.

The Morenos and Manuel and Fernando were the last to arrive. Soon they were drinking their fill of water and eating the kind of food that could be found only at the river.

Don Juan spoke to everyone and told them to rest for a few days, but then to prepare for a great feast and celebration of thanksgiving.

"You have been good and brave travelers, and you deserve to celebrate. We will hold a celebration on April thirtieth here on the banks of this great river. The feast will be a grand occasion."

And so it was. The day was bright and sunny. A gentle breeze swept through the cottonwood trees and made the leaves sing with the birds. Small cooking fires dotted the banks of the river. Horses and cows grazed peacefully on the nearby green meadow.

Don Juan told all the travelers to put on their best clothes for the great feast of thanksgiving. Soldiers polished their armor to perfection. Their horses were almost as shiny. Don Juan personally brought Manuel's and Fernando's clothes they had once returned. He even smiled at them and patted Captain-General on the head.

Then Don Juan stood on a small hill so everyone could see him and gave a long speech. Manuel and Fernando barely understood it, but they were told later that he had formally declared the land they had come through, the river, and the land to the north, as the possession of the King of Spain. And the name of his speech came to be known as "La Toma," or "The Taking."

Under a grove of trees there was a religious celebration, at which one of the participants was a Captain Farfan. Señor Zaldivar told the boys about him.

"He is a writer and has written a play about the experiences of crossing the desert. It will soon begin."

Manuel and Fernando had never seen a play. This one had lots of people in it, including several padres.

As the play ended, Don Juan de Oñate made another speech, not as long as his first one. Just before he finished, he raised his voice and called, "Manuel and Fernando Carrillo, please bring Captain-General Martinez and come up here beside me."

It was astounding. The crowd began to cheer in a roar that frightened the birds in the trees. Señor Zaldivar quickly came to them and pushed them forward to the stage.

"These young fellows and their goat have entertained you on your trip. Now I want them to really entertain you from this stage. They worked hard to bring you a little laughter, so show them how much you appreciate them.

"And one more thing," he added with a grin. "You must promise never to threaten this goat with the boiling pot. I have personally guaranteed his safety. Besides, we might need him on our next journey through the Paso del Norte. I have a feeling we're going to need laughter."

At that, everyone cheered.

And Captain-General Martinez rose on his hind feet and gave a magnificent *bleat-bleat*.

Then everyone turned toward the tables of logs that were heaped high with food. There were broiled fish, roasted ducks and geese. The six Indians who had frightened Manuel and Fernando brought more fish and wild turkey and javelina, and the cooks threw them on the great bonfire to roast.

One of Don Juan's cooks discovered a forgotten barrel of flour and made a sweet bread to be dipped in wild honey. And grapes and hackberries were gathered from nearby. It was truly a feast of thanksgiving.

With full stomachs and happy thoughts, Manuel and Fernando went to sleep that night alongside Captain-General Martinez. Before he dozed off, Manuel looked up at the clear, bright stars, and thought, Whatever is in store for us in the great adventure ahead, I am strong enough now to face. And for that, I am truly thankful. I don't need gold and silver or jewels.

# Historical Note

TWENTY-THREE YEARS before the 102 Puritans landed on Plymouth Rock, and perhaps twenty-four years before they celebrated a day that has come to be known as Thanksgiving, a much larger group of Europeans came to American soil and also held a feast of thanksgiving.

Some 7,000 horses, cattle, sheep and other domesticated animals comprised a four-mile long procession from New Spain (now Mexico) along with 400 people (including 135 families). These were the first European descendants who had a serious intent of colonizing in America. Their feast, like the New England one, also had Indian guests who contributed food. Like the Puritans, they had a very difficult and dangerous journey. Unlike them, the Hispanics traveled over dry — very dry — land, but it held as many perils as the ocean did for the Puritans.

Perhaps as important as the first major colonization of families in America was the "colonization" of domesticated animals, primarily the horse. The hardy little Mustang beast was ideally suited to desert terrain, and became the darling of Indians who had been only as mobile as their legs could carry them. Aside from an occasional stray from earlier, smaller explorations, Indians had not seen the animal that was to liberate the Comanches and Apaches into the most remarkable horse-and-man partnership ever known. Their impact on the settling of the west still affects our lives.

# ❖ Glossary and Pronunciation Guide ❖

**Berta**   BEAR-tah

**Carrillo**   kahr-REE-yo

**Chihuahua**   chee-WAH-wah. A city, the capital of Chihuahua, a state in northern Mexico. Also one of a breed of very small, short-haired dogs. In this book, however, Chihuahua refers only to the Chihuahuan Desert, which covers a vast area in northern Mexico, west Texas, and into southern New Mexico and an edge of eastern Arizona. The desert is distinguished by elevations ranging from 1,000 feet along the Rio Grande to 6500 feet in Mexico. It is defined as a cold desert because it receives snow and the temperature drops below freezing over 100 times per year during the winter at night. In summer the temperature soars to over 100 degrees, and ground temperatures can rise to 165 degrees. Average rainfall is between 7.8 and 12 inches per year. Included in the native plants (cactus, yucca, agave, and many others) is the lechuguilla (lech-oo-GHEE-yah), which grows only in the Chihuahuan Desert. (The saguaro [Sah-WAR-o] grows only in the Sonoran Desert.)

**Cholla**   CHOY-a. A cactus, spiny and treelike.

**Conchos River**.   KOHN-chos. Until Juan de Oñate's expedition, explorers traveled northeasterly from Mexico up the Conchos River to its confluence with the Rio Grande, then followed the Rio Grande west and north. Oñate elected to go straight north from near Santa Barbara. His trail is roughly parallel to what is now Mexico Highway 45 south of El Paso, Texas.

**Coyote**   ky-OTE-ee (or KY-ote); in Spanish, ko-YO-tay

**Don**   dohn. A title of respect for a man of importance.

**Farfan**   far-FAHN. Captain Farfan was a member of the Oñate expedition who wrote a play describing the crossing of the desert. It is now recognized as the first dramatic production in America, performed April 30, 1598, at a location near what is now San Elizario, a village about sixteen miles east of El Paso.

**Fernando**   fair-NAHN-do

**Juan**   HWAN

**Luis**   loo-EES

**Lupe**   LOO-pay

**Manuel**   mahn-WELL

**Martinez**   mar-TEE-nes

**Moreno**   mo-REHN-0

**Norte**   NOHR-tay. (See Paso del Norte)

**Ocotillo**   o-ko-TEE-yo. A desert plant with long slender spikes that produce scarlet blossoms.

**Plaza**   PLAH-za

**Rio Bravo, Rio del Norte, Rio Grande**. REE-yo, BRAH-vo, GRAHN-day. Strong river, river of the north, and big river; also Rio Bravo del Norte. All these names refer to the river known in the United States as Rio Grande, and in Mexico as Rio Bravo.

**Siesta**   see-ESS-tah. A nap, brief rest.

**Tia**   TEE-ah. Aunt. (Tio — uncle.)

**Tornillo**   tor-NEE-yo. A desert plant that produces edible beans known as "screw beans."

**Tortilla**   tor-TEE-ya. A thin, round unleavened bread prepared from corn meal, baked on a flat plate of iron, earthenware, or the like.

**Vicente**   vee-CEN-tay

**Viceroy**. A ruler of a country appointed by a sovereign (in Spanish, the word is "virrey").

**Yucca**   YUCK-a. A desert plant with pointed, usually rigid leaves that produces snow white blossoms. Most all parts of this plant were useful to early Indians and explorers.

**Zacatecas**   sah-kah-TAY-cas. A silver-mining city in north central Mexico.

**Zaldivar**   sahl-DEE-var

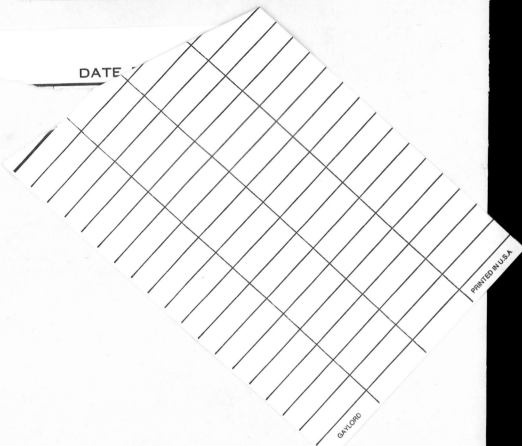

DATE

GAYLORD

PRINTED IN U.S.A.